The  Peppermint Lighthouse

by Frances T. Palmer

Illustrated by Julie H. Luther

Night and day, along the sea
the Peppermint Lighthouse sadly sat.
After many years of ocean winds,
teeming rains, blustering snowstorms,
and sea water spray, the
Peppermint Lighthouse had become
gloomy and drab.
It had lost its coat of paint...
it had lost its red peppermint
candy cane stripes... and its
shining beacon light had long since
been extinguished!!!

"I wish someday, someone would
notice me"...
said the Peppermint Lighthouse.

Spring soon awakened the
budding trees. As flowers poked their
dainty heads above ground, they did not
see the Peppermint Lighthouse.
The soft spring rains did not notice
the Peppermint Lighthouse.
Not even the ducks or geese flying
north for the spring season had noticed
the sorrowful Peppermint Lighthouse.

"Someday, maybe someone will notice me",
cried the Peppermint Lighthouse.

9

Along came summer!!
The boats and ships at sea
did not notice
the Peppermint Lighthouse.
Little children and their families
on vacation at the beach did not notice the
Peppermint Lighthouse.
Not even the lobsters and crabs,
the pelicans and seagulls or even
the whales and dolphins
noticed the Peppermint Lighthouse.

"I hope someday, someone will notice me!!"
said the dejected
Peppermint Lighthouse.

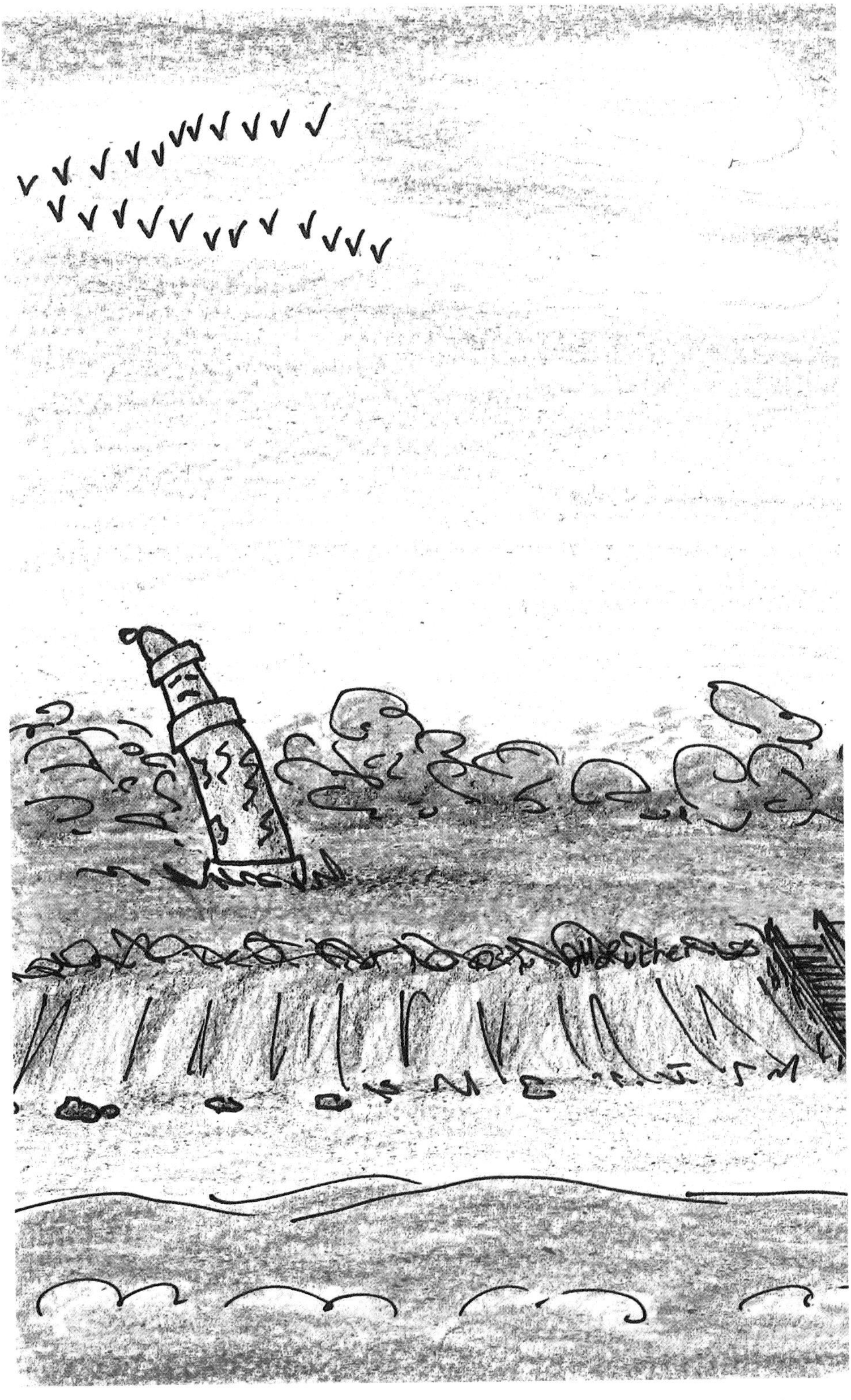

Summer turned into fall.
The colorful falling leaves and the
beautiful fall flowers gave no notice
to the Peppermint Lighthouse.
Blowing winds and pouring rains
did not notice the Peppermint Lighthouse.
Not even the geese and ducks flying south
for the winter noticed the
Peppermint Lighthouse.

"After all these years, will no one notice me?"
asked the downcast Peppermint Lighthouse.

When winter rolled along,
the evergreen trees growing tall for Christmas
did not notice the
Peppermint Lighthouse.
The blowing snow and sleet
did not notice and went right by
the Peppermint Lighthouse.
Even the icicles did not take notice
and did not freeze on the
Peppermint Lighthouse.

So, the mournful,
lonely Peppermint Lighthouse cried...
"No one will ever notice me!!!!"

21

Then, soaring overhead, someone heard the
Peppermint Lighthouse's grievous cry.
Santa Claus, on his yearly journey,
driving his sleigh pulled by
eight tiny reindeer, led by Rudolph,
heard the Peppermint Lighthouse.
As busy as he was on this Christmas Eve,
he had seen and heard
the Peppermint Lighthouse!

What could Santa do?

Santa Claus gave the Peppermint Lighthouse
a brand new coat of paint.

Santa Claus gave the Peppermint Lighthouse
dazzling red peppermint candy cane stripes.

Santa Claus gave the Peppermint Lighthouse
a new light.....

as big as a bright shiny Christmas Star
that lit up the whole sky.

And from that Christmas Eve forward,
everyone from near and far
noticed the bright, shining, beautiful
Peppermint Lighthouse by the sea,
day and night!

Author

Frances T. Palmer, born in Ellenville, has been an Elmira (in upstate New York) resident since she was a toddler. Educated in local schools, **Fran** attended Elmira College and is retired from Chemung County Support Enforcement Unit. **Fran's** interests are many: knitting (for Hospice and the Arnot-Ogden Medical Center), needlepoint, music (she plays accordion, piano, organ, drums and guitar), scrap-booking, wreaths, flowers, volunteering at Eldridge Park and Sperr Memorial Park. **Fran** and husband Neal are the parents of a grown son. **Fran** is also a consummate animal lover and adores her 7 cats.

Illustrator

Julie Hamlin Luther, an Elmira native, lives in Franklin, MA with her husband and 2 teen-agers, a daughter and a son. A graduate of Elmira College, with a studio art major, **Julie** is known in New England for her whimsical dog sculptures, toys, furniture and drawings. She is a successful breeder and exhibitor of champion Lhasa Apsos and most of her artwork revolves around her love of dogs.

Editor

Susan Howell Hamlin, has most recently edited *The Legend of Owenah and Newamee*. An Elmira College alumna, **Sue** is retired from Cornell's Veterinary College. She has written numerous articles and edited the book *Afghan Hounds in America*. **Sue** has three grown daughters and is also Julie's mother.